The Trapped Puppy

Holly Webb

Illustrated by Sophy Williams

LiTTLE TiGER

LONDON

For all the amazing volunteers who work for
Mountain Rescue teams around the world

LITTLE TIGER
An imprint of Little Tiger Press Limited
1 Coda Studios, 189 Munster Road, London SW6 6AW

Imported into the EEA by Penguin Random House Ireland,
Morrison Chambers, 32 Nassau Street, Dublin D02 YH68

www.littletiger.co.uk

A paperback original
First published in Great Britain in 2023

Text copyright © Holly Webb, 2023
Illustrations copyright © Sophy Williams, 2023
Author photograph © Charlotte Knee Photography

ISBN: 978-1-78895-566-9

MIX
Paper | Supporting
responsible forestry
FSC
www.fsc.org
FSC® C171272

The Forest Stewardship Council® (FSC®) is a global, not-for-profit
organization dedicated to the promotion of responsible forest management
worldwide. FSC defines standards based on agreed principles for
responsible forest stewardship that are supported by environmental, social,
and economic stakeholders. To learn more, visit www.fsc.org

10 9 8 7 6 5 4 3 2 1

Chapter One

Amelia peered through the long grass at the side of the footpath, hunting for Poppet. Mum and Dad had persuaded Amelia and her older brother, Luke, to come for a walk up the rocky hillside above their village. It was a sunny spring afternoon, and Amelia could hear birds chirruping in the bushes and a hawk calling overhead. The sun

was warming the back of her jacket
too – it was blissful.

"Poppet, where have you gone, silly?"
Poppet was still so small that
she disappeared sometimes,
hidden by the thick weeds

and grasses, until she bounced up
to see where she was going. Amelia
spotted the grass shivering slightly
before the little black-and-tan terrier
appeared for a second at the top
of her bounce and was gone again.

"Poppet!" she called, and the grass wobbled again before Poppet whooshed out and leaped all over her, whining happily and scrabbling at Amelia's leggings.

"Oh, you're such a good girl," Amelia murmured, crouching down to rub the puppy's ears and make a fuss of her. They'd had Poppet for a couple of months now but she was only just old enough to start going for longer walks with their Labrador, Mickey. It was so much fun being out with both dogs.

Mickey stopped sniffing at a clump of brambles and looked over at Amelia as if he thought this was a bit unfair. He hadn't gone running off through the grass and had to be called back. Why wasn't he getting all

the praise and fussing?
Luke noticed and
leaned over to run
his fingers along
Mickey's spine,
and the big dog
closed his eyes
and pointed his
nose up to the
sky. That was his
favourite place to be
scratched – it made him go all wobbly.

"Do you think the dogs need a rest?"
Amelia's dad asked, sitting down on
one of the large rocks by the edge of
the path. "I could do with some water.
Maybe a biscuit…"

Both Poppet and Mickey swung their
heads round hopefully to stare at him.

They knew exactly what biscuits were.

Mum laughed. "Well, you'll have to give them something now," she said, taking off her backpack and starting to hunt for snacks – for both people and dogs. "But it's definitely time for a break. We must have been walking for over an hour and this path's pretty steep."

"It's really hot," Amelia said, wriggling out of her backpack too – inside she had a bottle of water and the special collapsible dog bowl they always brought on long walks. She sat down in the grass and unfolded the bowl, pouring in a drink of water for Poppet and Mickey.

Mickey lumbered over at once but Poppet was still begging hopefully for treats, her paws up against Mum's knees.

"You've already had two," Mum scolded gently. "No, Poppet, look, I'm putting them away. More later."

Poppet slumped down sadly and then shook her ears and trotted over to the water bowl. There was plenty of room for both dogs to drink but she nudged up close against Mickey, barging him with her shoulder.

"Poppet, you're so bossy!" Amelia said, rubbing Mickey's ears to make up for it. "Isn't she, Mickey? She's stealing your water… It's not fair, is it?"

The big Labrador stretched himself out in the cool grass and panted gently. He loved long walks. He didn't usually go very fast, just kept plodding along, slow and steady, while Poppet raced around. The little terrier probably covered three times as much distance as he did because she zigzagged back and forth, sniffing at interesting smells, chasing butterflies and checking on Amelia and Luke. She was a little busybody, Dad said. The two dogs were very different but Amelia's family adored them both, and Poppet and Mickey were best friends, even after only a couple of months.

Now Poppet settled down next to her older brother, snuggling close against him and laying her dark nose on top of his golden paws. Mickey looked up at Amelia and she was almost sure he rolled his eyes.

"You love her really," she whispered, rubbing his ears again and scratching Poppet under the chin when the little dog nudged at her in a demanding way.

After a few more minutes' rest they set off on their walk again, but Poppet had definitely slowed down. She was trailing along next to Amelia, puffing a little.

"Did you wear yourself out?" Amelia asked, crouching down next to her. Poppet sagged down on the path, looking up at her hopefully. She whined and Amelia giggled.

"Shall I carry Poppet for a bit?" she called to her parents, who were further ahead with Mickey.

"Oh dear, has she given up?" Mum said, turning round to look.

"It looks like she doesn't want to go any further," Dad agreed. "Are you sure you can carry her, Amelia? She gets heavy after a while."

"I don't mind." Amelia took off her backpack again and pulled her waterproof out, tying it round her middle instead. Now there was just enough room in there for a small, demanding dog. Poppet sat up hopefully, peering into the open bag.

"Yes, that's a space for you," Amelia

told her. "Come on then." She opened the bag invitingly and Poppet hopped in, snuggling down gratefully inside.

"I wish someone would carry me," Luke said, with a huge yawn. "You said this was a short walk, Mum."

"Well, it is…" Mum glanced over at him apologetically. "I'd forgotten how much hard work this path is though. We haven't been up here for a while."

Amelia slung her backpack carefully back on to her shoulders, feeling Poppet shift her weight inside. There was a snorty sort of yawn and then the little dog settled down for a nap.

"It's beautiful up here, even if it's tiring," Dad pointed out. "Just look at the view back down to home." He pointed across the hillside to their village, nestled

15

in the valley, with the river running through the middle. It did look really pretty from this height. It made Amelia think of their grandad's model railway, with all the houses so perfect and neat.

She smiled to herself as she heard a wheezy little snore from inside her backpack.

Poppet napped comfortably curled up in the bag, rocking gently as Amelia walked along. The bag was warm and she fitted neatly on top of Amelia's sweater. She snorted a little and padded her paws against the side of the backpack, chasing after Mickey in her sleep.

Then at last she blinked, yawned hugely and sat up, peering out of the open top of the bag. She gave a loud yap, and then wriggled round and licked affectionately at the back of Amelia's neck.

"Oh! You're awake again! Good timing, Pops. We're on our way down now."

"Here, I'll get her." Luke carefully lifted Poppet out of the backpack and the terrier zoomed in a tight circle around their feet, sniffing happily at the fresh grass. The backpack had been a little bit stuffy.

"Careful!" Amelia stepped over her. "I'll trip over you. Come on, Poppet. This way, look."

Poppet pranced back down the path ahead of the children, stopping every now and then to investigate the huge boulders dotted across the hillside.

She felt bouncy and full of energy after her nap, and she trotted back to say hello to Mickey as well, scrambling around his paws and then darting right under the big Labrador's tummy.

Mickey nosed at her and went on walking, while Poppet shot off again. She'd spotted – yes, there at the base of the big rock – a stick! She tugged at it but grass and weeds had been growing over it for a while and it didn't want to budge. She pulled harder and growled at it but still she couldn't get the stick to move.

"Do you want it?" Amelia asked, coming up behind her, and Poppet gave a demanding yap. She watched approvingly as Amelia pulled at the stick.

"Oooof! I almost fell over. This had better be a good stick, Poppet."

Poppet scurried backwards, barking excitedly and giving little jumps of joy.

"Ohhhhh, do you want me to throw it?" Amelia called, giggling. "Do you want to fetch the stick?"

Poppet danced around in skittish little circles, desperate for Amelia to throw the stick. Then she raced across the short, springy grass as Amelia tossed the stick into the air. She could see it starting to fall now – she was nearly there, just a bit further – Poppet leaped joyfully into the air, snatching at the stick before it reached the ground. She landed triumphantly on all four paws, her tail wagging in delight. She'd done it! She galloped back to Amelia, dragging the stick, which was definitely longer than she was.

Amelia beamed at her. "You're so good at fetching! Clever girl, Poppet, good dog!" She took the stick gently from Poppet's mouth and pulled back her arm to throw it once more.

Poppet bounced with excitement, watching the stick in Amelia's hand – she couldn't wait to chase after it again.

Chapter Two

Amelia swung her arm back and hurled the stick across the grass. Poppet did an amazing acrobatic leap and once again seized it in mid-air, then landed and pranced jauntily back to Amelia, obviously showing off.

"We need to catch up with the others now," Amelia told her as she took the stick back and looked around

for a good direction to throw it in.
"It's starting to get a bit misty up here,
Pops. The clouds are coming down.
We should head home."

"Amelia, come on!" Dad called from
a little further down the sloping path.

"Coming! Just one more throw!"
Amelia yelled back. "You heard that,
Poppet. One more, then we've got
to go."

Afterwards, Amelia wasn't quite
sure how she did it – one moment she
was throwing the stick for Poppet to
fetch, just as she'd done so many times
before, and the next she was flat on her
back, staring up at the darkening sky.

"Amelia!" Mum hurried back up to
her. "What happened?"

Mickey was standing over her too,

a worried look in his dark eyes, and Amelia could hear heavy footsteps as Dad and Luke raced towards them. Had she blacked out for a moment? She didn't understand. She propped herself on her elbows, shaking her head a little. Mum helped her to sit up.

"It looked like you slipped," Mum said, peering into Amelia's eyes. "Just as you were throwing that stick – as if your feet went out from underneath you."

"Ohhh…" Amelia blinked and nodded. She remembered now. She'd been watching Poppet, already racing away before the stick left Amelia's hand – and then a loose stone must have turned under her foot. She'd felt as if the ground wobbled underneath her – and then she was lying there with all her breath knocked out.

"That was weird," she muttered hoarsely, coughing a little. She still felt as if her lungs didn't have much air in them. She reached up to rub Mickey's muzzle – he was staring

25

at her so anxiously she felt like she
needed to let him know she was OK.
And the soft fur and wiry whiskers
felt very comforting under her fingers.
Then she blinked.

"Hey… Mum, where's Poppet?"

"Off chasing that stick, I expect,"
Mum murmured. She still looked
really concerned. "Amelia, do you feel
dizzy or anything? I'm just wondering
if you banged your head – there are
so many big stones around."

"I don't think I did. I'm fine. I just
hit the ground hard and lost my breath,
that's all." Amelia struggled to her feet.
"Dad, can you see Poppet? She ought
to be back with that stick by now."

Dad grabbed Amelia's arm, steadying
her as she stumbled a bit. "Um… No,

I can't see her. Which direction did you throw the stick in? I think you should sit down a bit longer, love, you're all wobbly."

"I'm not!" Amelia said, more sharply than she meant to. Actually, Dad was right, she did feel a bit strange, but it didn't matter. Why was she the only person who was worrying about Poppet? Everyone in the family knew how brilliant their tiny dog was at fetching sticks. She should be back here by now, jumping energetically and trying to convince one of them to throw the stick for her, just one more time. Poppet never wanted to stop playing. But there was no sign of her at all.

Where had the puppy gone?

Poppet raced across the thin grass, looking back at the flying stick overhead. Amelia had thrown it further and higher this time. Poppet barked joyfully, loving the feel of the turf under her paws as she dashed after the stick. It was dropping down now, she just needed to go a little further. Poppet scurried forwards one more step.

Except there was nothing there to step on to. The ground had disappeared under her paws. Poppet scrabbled frantically at the edge of the grass but she was sliding backwards and she just couldn't cling on. She fell, whimpering in panic as she bounced and scraped down a rocky wall.

However hard she tried to cling
to the tiny ledges and crevices, she
just kept on falling – until at last she
bumped down on to a damp stone
floor, and lay there, dazed and aching.

"Dad, I'm fine. Please! But where's
Poppet?" Amelia swung round, pulling

against Dad, trying to see through the gathering mist. They really did need to be heading home before it got any worse. But there was no little black-and-tan dog galloping out of the grey-white haze towards them. "She hasn't come back! Poppet! Poppet, where are you?"

There was no sharp answering bark. Not even a whine, as if Poppet was truly lost. "Poppet, come on!" Amelia called out, her voice high and anxious now. "Poppet, are you stuck somewhere? Poppet!" That last cry was almost a wail, and now Mum and Dad and Luke were looking around worriedly too.

"I don't think the mist would be a problem for her," Dad muttered.

"She'd be able to sniff her way back to us. Amelia, which way did you throw the stick?"

"I don't *know!*" Amelia cried. "It was sort of that way." She pointed across the hillside, where the mist was thickening. "But it could have gone anywhere when I fell..."

"Just stay here a minute," Dad said. "Stay together. I'll go and have a look."

"But it's so misty – you can hardly see!" Mum shook her head. "You can't go wandering off."

"I won't go far," Dad promised. "And I'll take Mickey. Mickey, here boy. Let's put your lead on. You'll help me find Poppet, won't you? What's that silly little dog done now, hey?"

31

Mickey wagged his tail slowly, as though he wasn't really sure what was going on. Amelia thought he looked worried too. After that one quick wag, his tail settled straight down between his legs and his ears went flat. He knew something wasn't right. But he set off with Dad, poking his nose forwards as if he was trying to see over the misty hillside.

Amelia clung on to Mum, listening as Dad called for Poppet. The mist did

32

funny things to his voice – he seemed
to be all over the place, and it was a
shock when he and Mickey appeared
round the side of a huge rock.

"I can't see any sign of her,"
Dad said, frowning. "But I don't
understand how she's just disappeared.
All I can think of is that she was
hungry and decided to head home.
It's close to the time she gets fed and
you know how greedy she can be."

Amelia stared at him. "Poppet
wouldn't do that," she said slowly.
"She'd never go off on her own."

Dad sighed. "She's nowhere close,
Amelia, I promise. I've looked – you
must have heard me calling. Not a
squeak back from her."

"The mist's clearing," Luke said.

"Look – you can see the top of that big rock now, and we couldn't a few minutes ago. We should keep looking for a bit. I think Amelia's right. Poppet likes to explore a bit when we're walking but she doesn't go far. She's never tried to go home on her own before."

"I know it seems odd but it's all I can think of," Dad said. "OK. Let's all carry on looking for her and keep calling."

"We can't stay up here for much longer, though," Mum pointed out. "The mist's clearing but it'll be properly dark soon."

"But … but we can't just go home without Poppet," Amelia pleaded.

"Dad could be right, Amelia. She might be sitting outside our front door," said Luke.

"She'll probably be really cross with us," Dad said, trying to sound cheerful. But he wasn't very convincing.

Amelia swallowed hard. She kept waiting for Poppet to dance out from behind one of the big rocks, as though the little black-and-tan dog had been playing a trick on them the whole time. It was just the sort of thing she'd do… But deep down, Amelia knew that wasn't going to happen. Poppet had disappeared – and Amelia couldn't help thinking that it was all her fault.

Chapter Three

Dad was wrong – Poppet wasn't waiting for them back home. Even at the end of a long walk, everyone had sped up as they came down the lane towards the house, hoping to see a grumpy little black-and-tan dog sitting on the doorstep, half hidden in the dusk.

"She's not here," Amelia whispered miserably.

"She could still be on her way," Mum suggested, though she didn't sound very hopeful.

"We'd have gone past her then, wouldn't we?" Luke crouched down to stroke Mickey's ears. The big Labrador was looking around, confused. He'd kept stopping to look back all the way down the hillside, clearly worried that Poppet wasn't with them. He adored the little terrier, even though she bossed him around.

"Poppet!" Dad called. "Here, girl! Poppet!"

Everyone else joined in, Amelia too, even though she was sure Poppet was still up on the hillside somewhere. She wanted nothing more than to be wrong. She'd be so happy to spot the puppy racing towards them through the fading afternoon light.

Their voices died away, and at last Mum sighed and pulled the keys out of her backpack. "I'll put a message in the village group chat asking everyone to keep a look out for her. And we'll go back up the hill first thing tomorrow." She pushed the door open and then reached back to hug Amelia and Luke.

"Don't worry. We'll find her."

Amelia nodded. Of course they would. Wouldn't they?

Amelia's mum and dad spent most of the evening calling neighbours and friends, asking them to look out for Poppet. Amelia called Maisie, her best friend from school who lived in the middle of the village. Her dad was part of the volunteer Mountain Rescue team and he knew everything there was to know about the hills around the village, according to Maisie.

"Poor Poppet," Maisie said, and Amelia could hear how worried she was over the phone. "But it'll be OK,

Amelia. I bet you'll find her tomorrow. And of course I'll tell Dad. He'll keep an eye out too." There was a garbled noise behind her and Amelia heard her say, "I know it's late, but it's important. Amelia's puppy's missing, Mum! They don't know where Poppet is!"

They don't know where Poppet is. Amelia felt worse than ever – they were such bad dog owners. If only she hadn't thrown that stick.

She let out a little gasp, trying not to cry, as Maisie came back on the phone. "It'll be OK, Amelia! Don't worry," she said hopefully.

"She's lost because of me," Amelia whispered down the line. "She was chasing a stick I threw and then she just disappeared. It's all my fault."

"That's not true!" Maisie said firmly. Maisie was good like that. She was always very sure about things. Some people at school didn't like her – they said she was bossy, but Maisie didn't care. She never backed down. She didn't mind saying sorry if it turned out she was wrong though.

"It feels like it is." Amelia slumped against the sofa cushions.

"It was an accident. Just bad luck.

And you're going to do everything you can to find her tomorrow, aren't you? I'll help. It's a good thing it's the holidays."

"Thanks, Maisie." Amelia blinked away tears. "I'll call you in the morning, OK?"

"Maybe Poppet will even be back by then," Maisie said firmly. "Night, Amelia."

But Poppet wasn't.

Amelia woke up a lot later than she'd meant to the next day. She sat up in bed, feeling tired and stressed and trying to remember why – and then it all flooded back to her. *Poppet had disappeared! Was she lonely? Was she frightened? Maybe she was hurt?*

Amelia's bed felt very odd without

the little puppy curled up at the end of it. Mickey liked to sleep on the rug next to Luke's bed, and Amelia had always wished he'd sleep in her room sometimes too. But a couple of weeks after they'd first got Poppet, the puppy learned how to climb stairs and discovered Amelia's room – and Amelia's bed. She'd never looked back.

Amelia had lain awake for ages the night before, unable to fall asleep, and in the end she'd got out of bed and gone to her windowsill. She'd sat there looking at the dark mass of the hillside rising up against the stars, wishing and wishing for Poppet to be safe, for her to come home. Amelia didn't know how long she'd been staring out of the window but she just about remembered Mum finding her asleep on the sill and guiding her back to bed.

She shoved back the duvet and dashed downstairs. Mum had gone to work but Dad was in the kitchen, drinking tea and wearing his outdoor clothes.

"Hey…" He smiled at Amelia but he looked worn out.

"Is she back?" Amelia asked hopefully. Deep down she knew Dad would have told her straight away if Poppet was home, but a tiny part of her was still wishing it.

"Not yet, love." Dad gave her a hug. "I've been out looking for her this morning."

Amelia sniffed. "You must have got up really early," she muttered into his fleece.

"I wanted to get up the hill before your mum left for work. We'll all go again in a bit, shall we?"

There was a loud clumping sound on the stairs and Luke hurried into the kitchen in his pyjamas. "Did she

46

come back?" he asked, looking around desperately.

Dad shook his head. "You're up early for the holidays…" he said, trying to sound normal.

"Yeah, well… I was worried." Luke gave a sigh. "Can we go out and look for her?" Then he turned slowly round in the kitchen, his voice going sharp with fear. "Where's Mickey?"

"It's OK. He's sitting in the front garden, by the gate," Dad said, making a face. "He came out earlier with me to look for Poppet and he didn't want to come back down the hill at all. He wouldn't come in the house. I went to check on him a few minutes ago and he was still sitting there, whining for someone to open the gate for him."

"He wants to go and get Poppet."
Luke's voice sounded a bit wobbly. "He
doesn't understand why she isn't here."

Amelia pressed her hand across her
mouth. Somehow the thought that
Mickey needed Poppet back was the
worst thing of all.

Amelia, Luke and Dad trailed into
the house, slumping down around

the kitchen table. Mickey went to his water bowl and drank thirstily before collapsing wearily on to the big dog bed. They'd spent the morning walking round the village, calling for Poppet and telling everyone they met that she was missing, then they'd gone back up the hill to look there again after lunch. No one had seen so much as a glimpse of a little black-and-tan terrier.

"What do we do now?" Luke asked, staring down at his hands.

Dad got up to unzip his jacket. "I'm not sure yet. Ummm... Maybe I'll call the vet again, just in case. And when Mum rang from work earlier she said there's an animal shelter in Winsfield that we should check too."

"But Poppet's got your phone

number on her collar tag," Amelia pointed out. "If someone had found her they'd phone us, wouldn't they?"

Dad gave a sort of shrug and a nod at the same time. "Well, yes. But I don't want to miss any chance of finding her. You never know." He glanced up at a noise out by the front door. "There's your mum back from work." He got up and went into the hallway, closing the kitchen door behind him. Amelia and Luke could hear a low buzz of voices as he talked to Mum.

"I thought we'd have her back by now, for sure," Luke muttered, and Amelia nodded.

"I know. Where can she be, Luke? I don't get it."

The kitchen door swung open, and

Mum and Dad came in to sit down next to them. Mickey clambered out of his bed and came to rest his nose in Mum's lap. She ran his ears through her fingers, smiling sadly down at him.

"Listen, you two," Dad started, and Amelia caught her breath. That wasn't the kind of voice anyone used for good things. Dad stopped and swallowed. Then he started again. "We have to be – um – realistic about this. Of course we're going to keep looking for Poppet. But it's possible…"

"Possible what?" Amelia whispered, leaning forwards.

Dad exchanged a look with Mum and sighed. "There are all sorts of tunnels and holes left over from when there were lead mines around here. We have to accept that Poppet might have fallen into one of them."

"No!" Luke shook his head angrily. "No, that can't be right. They're all blocked up, those old mineshafts. I've seen them – they've got wire mesh across."

"They should be," Mum agreed. "But there are tunnels all over the hill, and every so often one of them opens up where no one's expecting it."

"But we'd have seen it, wouldn't we, when we went looking for her?" Amelia said, digging her nails into her palms. "How could we miss seeing a great big hole?"

"It might not *be* very big, that's the problem," Mum said. "And it was so misty, remember."

"We went back and looked up there today, though," Luke pointed out. Then his face crumpled. "I suppose we didn't mark exactly where she disappeared… We didn't know…"

"I don't understand," Amelia whispered. "What – what are you trying to say? That Poppet isn't coming back?" Dad reached out to put his arm round her but Amelia pulled away. "Don't! I don't want to hear it!" She stumbled up, pushing the chair back across the tiled floor with a shriek that made Mickey whimper. Then she darted upstairs and flung herself on to her bed. It couldn't be true. It just couldn't.

Chapter Four

Poppet stood up again, wincing
as she tried to put weight on her
twisted paw. She sniffed at it and
tried nibbling at the fur, but it didn't
seem to make it any better. She didn't
want to walk around – her paw hurt
so much and all she really wanted to
do was huddle up against the rocky
wall, where she felt safer. But she

was getting cold
again. She could
tell she needed
to move. She
peered up at
the tiny point
of light high
above and set
her front paws
up on to a
jutting piece of
stone. Perhaps,
once her paw
felt a bit better,
she could climb
back up there?
But the light
seemed a very long
way away.

Poppet barked, just once, and then shivered as her bark came back to her as a string of eerie echoes. She didn't like it. She tried again, whining instead, and that was worse – a faint whispering of whines all around.

Amelia and Luke would come and find her, she thought, gazing up at the light again. It was getting fainter now – grey-blue instead of white. The light was going away. She didn't want to be down here on her own in the dark again, without even that spot of light to look at.

Poppet forgot about the frightening echoes and howled, the sound coming back to her as a broken wail. She jumped down, gasping as her weight fell on to her hurt paw. Then she curled up against the damp rocks and shut her eyes tight. Now she couldn't tell if it was dark or not.

Both Dad and Mum were working the next day, and the plan was that Amelia was going to go round to Maisie's. Since Luke was fifteen, Amelia's parents let him stay on his own at home – which Amelia didn't think was very fair, but still.

Instead, Luke, Amelia and Maisie decided to stick together and try looking for Poppet again. Luke had his phone with him and he promised to keep calling Maisie's dad to let him know they were OK. Maisie's dad was working, but he promised he'd come and help them in the search for Poppet later on – he knew the hills really well. They were taking Mickey too – Amelia and Luke didn't want to leave him on his own at home. He was missing Poppet so much and he seemed really miserable.

"So where did you last see her?" Maisie asked as they headed up the hillside.

"I was playing fetch with her and she'd found a stick down the side of a big rock," Amelia explained. "I think I can find it again. It wasn't far away from the path."

"Look at Mickey," Luke said, pointing up ahead. They'd let the big Labrador off the lead – he was very good at coming back when he was called and he'd been so upset since Poppet disappeared, they'd wanted to cheer him up.

It hadn't been working. Mickey had just plodded along the path in front of them, his head hanging low – but suddenly he looked very different. His floppy Labrador ears couldn't prick right up, but Amelia could tell that they were set forwards now. Mickey was interested. His tail was swinging a little. He was sniffing too, tracking back and forth across the turf.

"Do you think he knows Poppet was here?" Amelia asked hopefully. "Has he smelled her, maybe?"

"Yeah, or perhaps he remembers that this is where we were," Luke agreed.

Amelia glanced around, frowning as she looked at the big rocks scattered across the hillside. Then she nodded eagerly. "Mickey's brilliant! That's the rock where Poppet found her stick, I'm almost sure." She hurried over to it, trying to remember the patterns of yellowish lichen growing across the stone. "Yes, it was definitely this one. So we were around here playing fetch… But we were sort of following you back down the hill at the same time."

"Further down then," Luke muttered, peering around and frowning. "Let's head back along the path a bit. Just be careful, all right? Mum wasn't that happy about me bringing you two up here. Watch out for any holes. You don't want to fall…"

Maisie rolled her eyes. "We're being careful. We're not three-year-olds."

"Shh," Amelia murmured. She wasn't really paying attention to them bickering. "I think we've gone too far? I don't think we'd walked this far down when she disappeared. Mickey! Come back here, boy!"

But Mickey wasn't listening. He was snuffling about in the long grass, his tail waving like a flag. He'd spotted something, Amelia was sure.

Or smelled it, maybe.

"It looks like he knows what he's doing..." she said to Luke and Maisie. "What have you found, Mickey?"

The three of them hurried over to him. Mickey was too busy to take much notice, but he did look up at them for a moment. His eyes were brighter – that worried fog had lifted and he looked alert, almost excited. Then he went back to tracking across the hillside and they followed.

"This has got to be past where we were," Luke said, glancing around. "We weren't anywhere near those rocks when you fell over, Amelia. Mickey's just sniffed out a rabbit or something..."

"Give him a chance," Amelia said

quietly, still watching the Labrador.
"Hey, look!"

Mickey had stopped by a cluster
of rocks that looked like they'd fallen
down the hillside a long time ago.
He was gazing up at them now,
proud and eager and excited.

Amelia raced towards the rocks. "He's found something!"

Poppet had woken up a few times during the night and each time she'd been surrounded by thick, solid darkness. She'd curled herself up into the tiniest ball and tried to shut herself away from it. But then, at last, she'd felt the darkness lift a little against her eyelids. There was the faintest bit of light coming down the rocky shaft. It was morning again. And perhaps her paw didn't hurt quite so much today? But she was so hungry… It was as if the pain from her paw had been distracting her

from wanting food. Now that she
was feeling a bit better, her insides
ached with hunger.
Poppet licked
at the large
puddle she'd
found – there
was moisture
dripping down
the wall, and
the water tasted
greenish and
mossy, but it was
better than nothing
– then she stood up, carefully testing
her paw. Just a twinge. She'd be fine to
walk on it for a bit, she thought. She
needed to find something to eat now.

Poppet started cautiously down the

narrow tunnel, sniffing hopefully here and there. She couldn't smell any food, only damp stone and earth, but there must be something. There had to be.

Poppet shook her ears briskly and trotted on.

Chapter Five

"I still don't think this is anywhere near the place Poppet disappeared," Luke argued, staring into the dark hole between the rocks. "We were much further up the hill. You know that, Amelia, you found the rock where Poppet got her stick!"

"Yes, of course I know that!" Amelia snapped. Then she took a deep breath and tried to calm down so she could explain properly, even though she felt like she was going to burst with fright and worry about Poppet. They needed Luke – they were only allowed to be up here on the hill because he was there too. Although if Luke got cross and said they had to go home right now, there was no way Amelia was going with him. Looking at Mickey, Amelia didn't think he would be either.

In fact, Mickey looked like he was about to go straight into that hole. "Hey! Grab on to him!" she gasped, reaching for Mickey's collar. She just about managed to catch the big Labrador before he disappeared into the hillside. Luke hurriedly clipped on a lead and pulled him back. Mickey

didn't want to come though. He was
still tugging eagerly, his tail wagging.

"What are you trying to do,
Mickey?" Luke said, making a fuss of
him. "Are you chasing rabbits? Silly
old dog…"

"I don't think he is, Luke, honestly!"
Amelia said. "Listen. If Poppet fell
down an abandoned mineshaft, doesn't
it make sense that there would be lots
of holes and tunnels all around here?"
She was speaking slowly, thinking it
out as she went along. "I know this isn't
where she disappeared, but it probably
all connects up underground, don't you
see?"

Luke looked round at her, frowning.
"Oh… You think Poppet's wandering
about down there? And Mickey's

sniffed out where she is now?"

"Yes!" Amelia nodded wildly. "Exactly!"

"Oh, that would be amazing," Maisie said. But then she peered anxiously into the dark hole. "But if Poppet's in there, how are we ever going to get her out?"

Amelia stepped closer. The hole looked like it might once have been the entrance to a tunnel, but it was half blocked with fallen rocks and earth. "I could get in there, I think," she said. It wasn't that she *wanted* to, exactly – the hole was dark and scary. But if Mickey thought Poppet was waiting for them down there, then she had to go inside.

"No way!" Luke grabbed his sister and pulled her back – hard enough that Amelia's arm hurt.

"Hey!" she snapped. "Don't grab me like that!"

"Sorry. I'm sorry, Amelia, I didn't mean to hurt you." Luke did look sorry and he patted her arm apologetically. "But you scared me! You can't go in there –  we've got no idea what's through that entrance. What if it's a straight drop and you fall down and break your leg or something?"

"I wouldn't," Amelia said stubbornly.

"Anyway, it's not like I was going to walk right in, I'd be really careful."

"How? It's dark, and we don't have a torch!"

"There's one on your phone!" Amelia pointed out.

Luke sighed. "Yeah, so we use up all my phone battery, then you get lost or a rock falls on your head and we can't even call Mountain Rescue. You're not going in there, Amelia, and you're *definitely* not taking my phone!"

Maisie sniggered and both of them swung round to stare at her. "Sorry. It just sounds a bit like you're more worried about your phone than you are about your sister."

Luke made a face. "Too right." But then he nudged Amelia and added,

"You know I don't mean that, don't you? Ooooof." He tugged on Mickey's lead again. "He really wants to get in there." Luke crouched down, putting his arm round Mickey's broad chest to hold him back. "Is Poppet down there, boy?"

Mickey turned his head, and his tail started to whip back and forth. He knew what Luke had just said, Amelia realized. Of course he recognized Poppet's name. Mickey licked his huge tongue all down the side of Luke's face, and then barked.

It sounded as if he was calling to Poppet.

"Yes, that's it! We should call her," Amelia gasped. "Maybe she'll hear us and come back out! Poppet! Here, Poppet! Come on, beautiful!"

"Poppet!" Luke and Maisie called, and Mickey barked again.

"Stop – give her a chance to bark back to us," Amelia hissed, waving at them both to shush. "Can you hear anything?"

"Not with you going on…" Luke

said, but then he stopped too, leaning as far as he could towards the hole in the rocks.

Amelia dug her nails into her palms, listening as hard as she could for any tiny sound coming out from the side of the hill.

Was that a scuffling noise?

A little whine?

"Did you hear that?" she whispered.

"What?" Maisie asked and Luke shook his head.

Amelia glanced at Mickey, who was sitting next to Luke now. He seemed the most relaxed he had been since they'd lost Poppet. His tail was wagging and he still looked hopeful. She was pretty sure that dogs had much better hearing than humans, as well as a much better sense of smell.

"Did you hear her?" she murmured, stroking the top of Mickey's head. The Labrador glanced over at her and panted happily.

"She's down there," Amelia said firmly. "I know she is and so does Mickey."

"Amelia…" Luke didn't sound cross. Actually, he sounded like Dad, Amelia realized. Dad when he had to say something that he knew was going to make them sad.

"She is!" Amelia folded her arms across her chest.

"I know you want her to be there – I do too! But – I think you're just hearing what you want to hear. You're imagining it."

Maisie sighed sadly and added, "I didn't hear anything either, Amelia. I'm really sorry."

"No..." Amelia whispered. She swallowed hard, trying to push down all the tears that had suddenly appeared. "Look at Mickey. He knows..." She stroked his head again, and Luke and Maisie did too. So they were all facing away from the hole when there was a strange little rattling noise – like a pebble falling – and a thin, faint cry echoed deep down inside the hill.

Amelia whirled round and Mickey sprang up, barking and barking.

"There! You heard *that*, didn't you?" Amelia cried. "Please tell me you heard it!"

Luke nodded, his eyes wide.
"Yeah..."

"Definitely," Maisie said with a gasp.
"Oh, Amelia, she's there!"

Poppet edged a little further along the
tunnel, sniffing her way cautiously.
She hated to be walking away from
the light but she was still desperate to
find some food – and a way out. She
could hardly see anything in the thick
darkness, so she was moving mostly by
smell. It felt like she'd been plodding
along in the cold forever. It was
horribly lonely.

She came to a place where the
passage opened out a little and she

smelled something that might be food
– not good food, but at least something
she could eat. She put her paws up
against the rocky wall and nibbled at
a mossy plant. It was bitter and dry
and she didn't like the taste, but it was
better than nothing.

There was a faint
scratching noise
in front of her
and a scuttling
movement in
the darkness.
Poppet jumped
forwards with
a sharp snap of
her teeth. A beetle
– all hard crackly wing
cases. She gobbled it down. Then she

realized – she had *seen* that beetle move, not just heard it. There was light again!

The wider passage forked away in several directions now and there was light coming from some of the tunnels – just the very faintest wisps of light, far away. Poppet sniffed at each opening, unsure which to choose. Did it matter? She sped up, hurrying hopefully along a narrow path towards the glimmering light. Perhaps she would even be able to get out?

"Poppet..."

Poppet stopped, frozen. Had she really heard that? Was it just another of those strange sounds that echoed though the tunnels, the sounds that had frightened her so much the night before? She shivered as an eerie barking whispered towards her.

But – she knew that bark.

It was Mickey!

They'd come back for her! They were looking for her! Poppet whined eagerly, scurrying along the passage, trying to follow the voices and the barking. She was going to see Amelia, Luke and Mickey!

But then the sounds began to fade. Poppet stopped, listening uncertainly. Why was the noise getting further away? She could hardly hear them now. Poppet yapped in panic, skittering first one way along the tunnel and then the other. Where were they? Had they left her behind again? Was she going in the wrong direction?

Silence. Poppet couldn't hear them calling for her at all any more. She'd missed them, missed her chance.

Poppet sank down on the stony floor and howled.

Chapter Six

"She's really there," Amelia whispered. "I wasn't sure we were ever going to see her again! Hang on, Poppet, we're coming!"

"No, we're not." Luke shook his head grimly. "We know she's there but that still doesn't mean you're climbing into that hole. It's not safe."

Amelia stared at him. "But – but she's

there! She's alive, Luke! We've got to get her out!" She swallowed hard. "We don't know how much longer Poppet can last down there. She hasn't had anything to eat. She might be hurt."

"She's getting out, don't worry," Luke said. "*We* can't do it though. Think about it. We need Mountain Rescue, or somebody who knows what they're doing! Not us messing around, Amelia. We're only going to make it worse."

"We need my dad!" Maisie yelped. "Luke, phone him! He's one of the Mountain Rescue volunteers."

"Will they rescue a dog?" Amelia asked anxiously. "Maybe it's only for people?"

"No, it's everyone. Dad's told me about rescuing all sorts of animals – lots of sheep, they're always getting stuck in places! But definitely dogs, don't worry." Maisie frowned. "I'm not exactly sure how he's going to get down there though."

They all looked at the dark space in the hillside – Maisie's dad was really tall, with huge shoulders. He *definitely* wasn't getting through there.

"He'll work it out somehow," Maisie said, and some of her sunny confidence rubbed off on Amelia too. She threw her arms round her friend and hugged her tight. "Poppet's going to be OK!"

Luke had pulled his phone out of his jacket pocket and was calling Maisie's dad. "Hi, Mr Williams. No, it's OK, we're fine. Better than fine! We've found Poppet – or we think we have.

We've heard her but she's stuck in an underground tunnel and we can't get at her, not safely anyway. Maisie said to call you because you're in the Mountain Rescue team?"

Amelia and Maisie leaned closer to try and hear what Maisie's dad was saying, but they could only catch a bit of it.

"… bring the car up … quicker … with you in half an hour …"

They beamed at each other and Amelia hugged Maisie again.

"Thanks!" Luke ended the call and sighed with relief.

"He's going to call a few of the other volunteers and

drive up the lane – he should be able to get close to us by car. Half an hour, he reckons!"

It wasn't even half an hour in the end, but it felt much, much longer to Amelia. It was so hard knowing that Poppet was stuck down there somewhere and that the waiting would be even more difficult for her. She kept calling down to Poppet, trying to reassure her, but they couldn't hear the little dog now. By the time Maisie's dad and the rest of the rescue team arrived, Amelia could hardly keep still.

"Dad!" Maisie called, waving excitedly as she spotted them hurrying along the path, loaded with equipment.

"We've left the Land Rover just back there," her dad said, giving Maisie as

much of a hug as he could round the pile
of ropes he was carrying. He grinned
at Amelia and Luke. "Well done for
finding her – you must be so relieved."

"We can't get to her though," Amelia told him anxiously. "Look! It's such a tiny space. I could get in there, maybe? But I don't think you can." She looked at the other Mountain Rescue volunteers – two men and a woman. None of them looked like they'd be able to fit through the opening in the hillside.

"This isn't where she got in," Luke explained. "That was further up the hill, we're pretty sure, but we can't find the hole. We reckon maybe there are lots of tunnels linked up under here? She could have been wandering around all over the place."

Amelia gulped. It was so hard to imagine poor Poppet, lost under the hillside, with no idea how to get out –

or whether anyone was coming to find her. She really hoped the little dog had heard them shouting. That she knew they were on their way at last.

Maisie's dad peered into the hole and then looked thoughtfully at the fallen rocks scattered around. "I reckon this mineshaft has been hidden by the rocks," he said, glancing back at the rest of the team. "It looks pretty fresh, doesn't it? Maybe there's been some movement underground, which could have caused a landslide here and opened up some other entrances at the same time."

"I've not seen it before," the woman volunteer agreed – and Amelia blinked, realizing she looked familiar. She was one of the teaching assistants at school. She'd not worked in Amelia and Maisie's class but Amelia thought she was called Miss Jennings. "It's got to be recent. We should probably get some warning signs put up nearby, do you think?"

Amelia glanced between them as they chatted, squeezing her fingernails into her palms. She wanted to tell them to stop wittering on about signs and get Poppet out of there!

"How are you going to rescue Poppet?" she blurted, and the rescue team looked round at her.

Maisie's dad sighed. "Good question. If we can't find another entrance to these tunnels – and there must be one, somewhere – then we might have to widen this one instead.

That could be tricky, though – the rocks have been falling around here already. We don't want to cause another accident."

Miss Jennings nodded. "We're not quite sure where Poppet is now either, are we? If she's not keen to come to us, we could end up wandering around under there for ages."

"Dad!" Maisie yelped. "I've had an idea! Why don't you use your drone!"

Amelia blinked at her. She knew what a drone was – Luke had got one last Christmas, a tiny one with a remote control. He'd had a lot of fun flying it, but then it had gone up too high, out of sight, and somehow he'd lost track of it completely. He'd looked for it for ages but Mum said it was probably stuck in a tree somewhere, or else it had been eaten by a sheep.

How on earth was a drone going to help Poppet?

But Maisie's dad was nodding. "Yes... You could be right, Maisie. I've got a drone for taking aerial photos," he explained to everyone else, and Amelia remembered that he was a photographer. He took their school photos. "It's got a camera on it, and I can see what the drone camera's seeing on my phone. We could use it to look for Poppet – and maybe find another way for us to get down into these tunnels too. I'm not positive the GPS tracker will work underground, but we can hope." He smiled at Amelia. "I've been practising my flying, and I'm sure I can get the drone through that hole."

Poppet lay on the stony ground, her chin resting on her paws. She was still very hungry but she couldn't summon up the energy to move just now. She'd been so excited when she thought she heard Amelia calling her and Mickey barking. Excited and hopeful. She'd thought she was getting out of this terrible damp dark place at last. Poppet had raced to find them, scampering down many different tunnels, but she'd taken a wrong turn somehow and the calling voices had faded away.

They had been there, hadn't they?

She'd been so sure… But now she couldn't hear anything, anything at all. Even her own breathing sounded thin and whispery and quiet. Perhaps she'd thought Amelia was calling to her but it had only been those strange echoes again?

What was she going to do now? She couldn't just stay here. She had to do *something*… Wearily, Poppet lifted her head and peered along the tunnel. It was almost completely dark in both directions. She couldn't tell where the hole she'd first fallen through was – there was no sign of the light shining down.

She had to pick a way and keep going. If she did that, maybe she'd find Amelia and Luke and Mickey. She'd never find them if she didn't move, would she?

Poppet dragged herself to her feet and padded along the corridor. One paw after another. She mustn't stop, because if she stopped, she might give up.

Chapter Seven

Two of the rescue volunteers went off to scout for other ways into the abandoned mine tunnels and Miss Jennings stayed with Amelia, Maisie and Luke – but she told them to call her Sally, since they weren't at school. Then Maisie's dad came back from the car with a small black carrying case, which he unzipped to show them all the drone. It looked a little bit like a tiny helicopter but with four sets of rotor blades, one on each corner.

"It's all charged up," he explained. "We should have about half an hour's flying time on this battery. It would be more, but we'll need the light on, and that runs the battery down faster."

Amelia nodded. Half an hour. It didn't sound very long. She watched as Maisie's dad slotted his mobile phone into a holder on the remote control and powered up the drone. The view from the camera underneath appeared on his phone screen – just a close-up of grass at the moment. But then there was a thin, eerie buzzing and the drone lifted off the ground and hovered, and a light came on, shining down from underneath.

"Looks good," Maisie's dad murmured. "OK. Let's see what we can see!"

He moved the buzzing drone towards the narrow hole in the hillside, and carefully guided it inside, watching the drone but glancing back at the phone screen every so often. Amelia gazed hopefully at the phone. It was hard to tell exactly what the camera was seeing at first but then she worked out that the drone was flying very slowly downwards, between rough stone walls.

"I think this must have been an access tunnel once," Maisie's dad said. "Looks like it's a pretty gentle slope. People could have walked down it…"

"Do you think Poppet could climb back up this way, then?" Luke asked.

"Possibly… We'd need to get her to the right place, of course. Ah! We're flattening out now. Lots of fallen rocks around. And I suppose these bits of wood must have been props holding the roof up."

"Have they fallen down?" Maisie asked, peering round his arm. "There's a lot of wooden bits on the ground."

"Rotted away, I should think," Sally said. "These old lead mines haven't been used for about two hundred years. That's why it's so risky going anywhere near the tunnels."

Amelia felt Maisie reach out and take her hand and she smiled weakly at her friend. Poppet was wandering around down there in tunnels that could collapse at any moment…

"It'll be OK," Maisie whispered. "Dad's going to find her."

"I think we're at a sort of crossroads

here," Maisie's dad murmured. "Several different ways to go – oh!"

"What?"

"What happened?"

"Did you see something?"

Everyone was talking at once and trying to see the phone screen without accidentally jogging Maisie's dad's arms.

"I think I saw her! It was just a flash – something moving along one of the side tunnels. I mean, don't get too excited. It could have been a bat startled by the light or maybe a rat…" He moved the control toggles carefully and Amelia stared at the tiny phone screen, biting her bottom lip.

"There!" Maisie's dad whispered. Then he chuckled to himself. "I'm whispering so as not to scare her but she's nowhere near us, of course." He turned the screen more towards Amelia and Luke. "Can you see her?"

The screen was showing the same dark rock walls, flecked with lighter crystals here and there. But further along in front was a small shape, a bit blurry in the strange light. It was definitely Poppet though – Amelia could see her tawny paws, and even the pale tufts above her eyes that looked just like eyebrows. Usually they made Poppet look a bit surprised – but right now the little dog's eyes were wide, and scared. She obviously had no idea what the drone was.

It was hard to tell on the screen but Amelia thought that Poppet was trembling.

"She's backing away…" Maisie's dad said, whistling between his teeth.

"Oh, Poppet…" Amelia whispered, watching her scurry away from the drone. "No, please come back! She's going further in!"

"It's OK, Amelia." Sally darted a quick smile at her and Luke and Maisie. "Try not to worry. She doesn't look as though she's hurt and she's not that far away from us."

"Should we try calling her again?" Amelia suggested.

"Let me get the drone back out first," Maisie's dad said. "She definitely looked scared when it was close to her. She might be confused if she hears you calling and sees the drone. I'm getting low on battery too – but I've got another one in here, don't worry." He frowned, wrinkling up his nose as he concentrated on piloting the drone back out of the tight cluster of rocks around the entrance. Amelia could hear the high-pitched buzzing as it flew towards them. She could understand why Poppet had been scared – she'd have no idea what this strange thing was, buzzing around in the silent tunnels.

"OK," Maisie's dad said as the drone settled slowly on to the grass. "So we know Poppet's there and she's definitely well enough to move around. And the tunnel that leads up to this entrance looks as if it should be fine for her to walk up. Last time we saw her she was in one of the tunnels that branches off the open area – the one that leads to the right, and she was heading away from us." He sighed. "I suppose the light must have been a bit scary too, thinking about it. So how are we going to get her back to us?"

"Dan and Kiran radioed and said they haven't found any other entrances," Sally said. "They're on their way back. I suppose the tunnels were blocked up on purpose, to stop anyone getting in."

"So – we have to get Poppet out this way?" Amelia asked.

Maisie's dad nodded. "I think so. If we can't bring her to this tunnel, we'll have to see if we can widen the entrance so we can send rescuers down to get her. That's a last resort though." He nodded towards the huge rocks that had fallen around the entrance. "It would be a big job. Why don't you two try calling her again?" he suggested to Amelia and Luke.

Amelia went closer to the rocks, glancing up cautiously. Nothing looked as if it was about to fall on her, but still... "Poppet! Here, girl! Poppet! Come on, Poppet!"

Luke joined in and Mickey barked
hopefully too. Then all three of them
stopped and listened. Amelia was
sure she could hear her own heart
thumping in the silence.

But not a sound came from down inside the tunnels.

Poppet stood pressed against the rock wall, breathing fast. The buzzing thing was gone, she was almost sure. She couldn't hear it – and she couldn't feel that strange fluttering in the air any longer. It had been chasing her, but then it headed off down one of the tunnels. Poppet shivered. She was staying well away from there. That bright, glowing light had made her eyes hurt after so long in the dark.

"Poppet!"

The little dog's ears pricked up. That was Amelia! And yes, there was

Luke too. She could even hear Mickey barking. They hadn't left her after all!

She scurried forwards again, determined not to lose them this time. At the edge of the tunnel, where it opened out, she stopped and peered cautiously around the fallen stones. The buzzing thing had headed off in this direction, but even the joy of hearing Amelia and Luke and Mickey hadn't taken away her fear of the strange machine.

"Come on, Poppet!"

She crept a little further out into the open space, her ears laid flat against her head. What if it came back? What if it was here somewhere, waiting for her?

But she could hear them – they were

close, she was sure of it. They were telling her to come. What was she going to do?

Chapter Eight

"Poppet! Come on!" Amelia tried again. "Good girl, come on, Poppet!"

"Maybe she's too far away to hear us," Luke said. He looked at Maisie's dad. "I was hoping you could guide her out with the drone but she's obviously scared of it."

"She must be so hungry by now," Amelia said miserably. "Two whole days and she hasn't eaten. Oh! I brought her dog treats. Perhaps we could throw them in through the hole and she'd come up and get them? Do you think she'd sniff them out?"

"It's worth a go," Maisie's dad agreed.

Amelia pulled the packet out of her backpack and scattered a handful as far into the hole as she could reach. "Poppet! Snacks!" she called. "Come on, you love these ones," she added, her voice wobbling a little. She glanced round at Mickey, expecting to see him watching her eagerly for his own share, but the big Labrador was sitting solemnly next to Luke, gazing into the hole in the hillside. "If Poppet heard me throwing treats,

she'd be racing up here now. I wish
we could get them further inside –
can I go in, just a little bit?"

"No!" Luke, Maisie's dad, Sally and
even Maisie all snapped at almost
exactly the same time, and Amelia
sighed. She glanced at Maisie's dad.
"Can the drone carry things?"

He blinked at her. "What, like dog treats?" He looked down at the carrying case. "It's not a bad idea, I'm just not sure how we'd do it. There's no way to fix on a packet, or anything. Although…" He turned round, looking across the hillside to the lane where the rescue team had left the car.

"What is it, Dad?" Maisie asked, after they'd all stared at him for a moment.

Maisie's dad suddenly smiled. "Don't laugh, but I've got a packed lunch with me in the car – I was going to go and do some drone shots later on. There's a couple of rolls with sausages in. What if we put a sausage on a string and tied it to the drone? Would Poppet go for a sausage, Amelia?"

Amelia nodded, giggling. "She nicked a sausage off Dad's plate once! She was so quick – he got up to get a drink and she jumped on his chair and grabbed it, and it was gone in seconds! I've never seen anyone eat so fast!"

"Can you really tie it to the drone?" Luke asked.

"Well, to be honest, I've never tried flying the drone with anything tied to it," Maisie's dad admitted. "But I don't see why it wouldn't work. We'll need to try and keep the drone balanced, so the string will have to go round the middle, otherwise it won't fly." He grinned. "I'll go and get my lunchbox."

While Maisie's dad was away, Amelia stood by the hole talking to

Poppet. She knew the puppy probably couldn't hear her but it still helped her feel better.

"Maisie's dad's gone to get you a treat, Poppet. You know you love sausages. Remember how Dad was so cross when you stole half his dinner? He said you were a little menace… But he does really love you. We all do. We've been so worried…"

"He's coming back!" Maisie called. "Have you got any string, Dad?"

"Yup, luckily there was a ball of string in the tool box in the car," her dad said, holding it up. He handed it to Luke, together with a penknife and a big plastic lunchbox. "Cut off a long piece of string for me and tie it round one of the sausages in there.

117

I'll get the drone out."

Luke carefully looped the string around one of the sausages and then they tied the other end round the drone.

Maisie's dad picked up the remote control. "OK. Moment of truth, let's see if we can get this thing to fly." He turned the drone on and it started to buzz as everyone watched anxiously to see if it would get off the ground.

"Somebody needs to take a photo of this," Maisie's dad said, looking at Luke as the drone went up, pulling the string taut and then lifting so the sausage dangled in the air. "I can't believe I'm piloting a flying sausage."

"It's working!" Amelia said. "Oh, I hope Poppet follows it."

"She's not going to be able to resist," Luke said confidently.

Amelia nodded, crossing her fingers as the drone headed through the opening into the mine, lurching a bit, with the tempting snack swaying slowly underneath.

Poppet peeped out into the opening between the tunnels. She was still listening for the buzzing machine, but she was sure that she could smell fresher air coming down one of the tunnels. There were familiar scents on that air too, scents of home. She could smell Amelia and Mickey and Luke.

And food. There was *definitely* a food smell out there. Poppet sniffed hopefully, feeling her mouth water. She was so hungry, she couldn't remember the last time she'd had anything to eat – apart from tiny mouthfuls of bitter-tasting moss.

Poppet tucked her tail between her legs and scurried forwards, keeping low to the ground in case that thing flew over her again. She couldn't go too fast – even though the space was open, it was littered with fallen rocks and bits of wood. She had to pick her way carefully through in the darkness.

This tunnel was lighter, Poppet realized as she reached it. Perhaps it led to a way out! She padded on, sniffing at the cleaner air, and slowly watching the stony walls around her grow clearer in the faint light.

Then she froze. That noise – a soft, insistent buzzing – the machine was back! Poppet whimpered, huddling down by the side of a larger rock. She could see it now, the bright light blazing as it charged towards her, faster this time. Poppet wanted to run, but she was too scared to move. The buzzing machine stopped just in front of her, hovering – but this time something was different. Poppet peered round the side of the rock. That food smell was even stronger – there was food hanging from the buzzing thing! Food that smelled familiar and delicious… Poppet crept out a little, trying to see better, and the machine pulled back, further up the tunnel.

Poppet's whiskers twitched. It was moving away from her now! But then so was the delicious-smelling food.

She trotted along after it, watching the sausage swaying on the end of its string. The smell was so good… She sped up a little and then reached out, snapping at the treat. The buzzing machine jerked and pulled away faster.

"Poppet! Oh, Poppet, you're there! That's it, Poppet, come on!"

Poppet's ears pricked up. Amelia!

There was a joyful woof up ahead and Poppet charged past the drone and along the tunnel, abandoning the sausage. They were there, waiting for her!

"She nearly downed the drone," Maisie's dad said, fiddling frantically with the controls. "I didn't think about what would happen if she grabbed the sausage and pulled on the string. Luckily she missed."

"She's coming out," Luke said excitedly. "Hey, I can hear her!"

A whining, wagging, black-and-tan bundle came darting out of the hillside. Poppet flung herself at Amelia, then Luke, then Mickey, again and again, so excited that she couldn't decide who she wanted to say hello to most.

"You're OK!" Amelia said, half laughing, half crying. "We thought we were never going to find you! Oh, Poppet, don't ever do that again, please."

"Here." Maisie's dad broke the sausage in half to get it off the string and handed the pieces to Amelia. Poppet gobbled them down and licked Amelia's fingers all over.

"Oh wow, she inhaled that, didn't she?" Maisie's dad laughed.

Mickey leaned over and sniffed at Poppet as if he was trying to work out where the sausage had gone.

"Sorry, Mickey…" Amelia murmured. "On the way home we'll stop at the shop, we can get sausages for both of you!" She looked up at Maisie's dad and the other volunteers. "Thank you for getting her back for us!"

"Lucky we had the drone!" Maisie's dad said, smiling. "I'm just glad it worked out."

"I've texted Mum and Dad and told them we've found her," Luke said, reaching down to rub Poppet's ears. His phone pinged. "Oh, Mum says she's crying because she's so happy."

"Me too," Amelia whispered as Poppet nuzzled against her cheek. Poppet's chin was velvet-soft and furry, studded with prickly little whiskers. Amelia could feel Poppet's tail too, thudding contentedly against the sleeve of her jacket. She stood up carefully, cradling the puppy in her arms.

"Come on, Poppet. Let's go home."

HOLLY
WEBB

Holly Webb started out as a children's
book editor and wrote her first series for
the publisher she worked for. She has been
writing ever since, with over one hundred
and fifty books to her name. Holly lives
in Berkshire, with her husband and three
children. Holly's pet cats are always
nosying around when she is trying
to type on her laptop.

For more information
about Holly Webb visit:

www.holly-webb.com